The President Is Dead

The ONCE UPON AMERICA® Series

The President Is Dead

A STORY OF THE KENNEDY ASSASSINATION

BY VIRGINIA T. GROSS

ILLUSTRATED BY DAN ANDREASEN

VIKING

Thanks to
L. J. Hofschneider, Jr., and Dr. Edward Rincón,
who helped me visualize Dallas, Texas,
and to Arlene Wilson
for providing the flavor of Mexico.

VIKING
Published by the Penguin Group
Penguin Books USA Inc., 375 Hudson Street, New York, New York 10014, U.S.A.
Penguin Books Ltd, 27 Wrights Lane, London W8 5TZ, England
Penguin Books Australia Ltd, Ringwood, Victoria, Australia
Penguin Books Canada Ltd, 10 Alcorn Avenue, Toronto, Ontario, Canada M4V 3B2
Penguin Books (N.Z.) Ltd, 182–190 Wairau Road, Auckland 10, New Zealand

Penguin Books Ltd, Registered Offices: Harmondsworth, Middlesex, England

First published in 1993 by Viking, a division of Penguin Books USA Inc.
1 3 5 7 9 10 8 6 4 2
Text copyright © Virginia T. Gross, 1993
Illustrations copyright © Dan Andreasen, 1993
All rights reserved

LIBRARY OF CONGRESS CATALOGING-IN-PUBLICATION DATA

Gross, Virginia T.
The President is dead : a story of the Kennedy assassination / by
Virginia T. Gross ; illustrated by Dan Andreasen.
p.   cm. — (Once upon America)
Summary: On November 22, 1963, Bernardo skips school in order to
see his idol, John F. Kennedy, in person, only to witness the
unthinkable—a presidential assassination.
ISBN 0-670-85156-6
1. Kennedy, John F. (John Fitzgerald). 1917–1963—Assassination—
Juvenile fiction. [1. Kennedy, John F. (John Fitzgerald),
1917–1963—Assassination—Fiction.] I. Andreasen, Dan, ill.
II. Title. III. Series.
PZ7.G9043Pr 1993   [Fic]—dc20   93-14888 CIP AC
Once Upon America® is a registered trademark of Viking Penguin, a division of
Penguin Books USA Inc.   Printed in U.S.A.
Set in 12 pt. Goudy Old Style

This book is lovingly dedicated to
Bernard F. Gross,
who, with honor, guarded the precious
remains of John Fitzgerald Kennedy
during the dark morning hours of
November 23, 1963.

Contents

Kid from
the Village

Bernardo's secret buzzed inside him like a bee against a window. He had told no one, not even Santo, his closest friend. If Santo knew, he'd want to be part of it, and this was a plan for one only. Two would make it too tricky. It might not work with two.

All week long, Bernardo polished his idea, fixing up the weak spots, making it doubly safe. He planned exactly what he would do and how to cover his tracks after doing it.

He counted the time. Four more days. Three more

days. Two. One. Now the day was here. He was ready.

It was early, still dark. Bernardo lay in bed, wide awake. Mama would think it strange if he got up now. She would ask questions when she came in to wake him up. He didn't want to start the morning with lies. Better to pretend to be sound asleep.

Below his window, Papa's old 1953 Chevy wheezed and coughed. The car was ten years old this month. Papa had bought it the day Bernardo was born.

He had spent all the family's savings in one day. "I had to have something fine for my son," he told Mama at the hospital.

Mama was mad! "What's this? Do you think we're rich Anglos? We live in Little Mexico Village, remember?" Nurses smiled at each other and looked away.

Papa paid no attention. "Our son is born American," he said happily. "New cars are American! Every Latino in the Village will look at this car and know that things are better somewhere." But never again had there been enough money to buy a whole car in one day.

Bernardo turned over in bed. He imagined his father leaving the house, his white pants looking spooky in the light from the streetlamp. A clean, starched apron would be folded on the backseat of the Chevy. It was a ten-minute drive to the Tortilla Kitchen, Papa's small restaurant in central city. There he served the best Mexican food in Dallas.

Bernardo loved the restaurant. Each October, when the State Fair came to Fair Park, all the excitement of Texas passed through its doors. And in the fall, the Cowboys played football in the Cotton Bowl. Win or lose, Papa's Mexican Bar-B-Q was what people wanted when the game was over.

It was after a game, one week ago, that Bernardo had first heard the news. Three men and a police officer came into the restaurant. The men looked different from the regular football crowd. They wore suits and ties. All they ordered was coffee.

Bernardo knew from their faces and voices that something big was going on. "Papa, what are those men talking about?" he had asked.

Papa smiled. "You're in fifth grade and still you do not know that soon the President of our country will pay Dallas a visit?"

"President Kennedy?"

Papa mussed Bernardo's hair "Ah. You do know something!" he teased. Bernardo hardly heard the teasing. He stared at Papa. These men were planning the President's visit! Jack Kennedy, right here in Dallas!

Kennedy was the hero of the Village. The day he was made president, he talked about a New Frontier, a better world. If anyone needed a better world it was

the crowded, poor, Latino families who had come into Bernardo's neighborhood from Mexico. They came looking for work. They wanted to be American.

After school the next day, walking to the restaurant, Bernardo had heard a familiar voice. "Hey! Chicano!" His fingers curled inside his fists. He didn't look around.

He knew it was James. James Cleary, one of the few Anglos who lived in the Village and went to St. Anna's school. James Cleary hated living in the Village. He hated going to St. Anna's. He hate Latinos and he hated Bernardo. Bernardo hated him back.

The voice came nearer. "What's the matter, Chicano. You chicken?" The anger in Bernardo's stomach burned away the fear. He *wasn't* a Chicano! Mama and Papa were born American, and so was he. He stopped.

James, a year older and a head taller than Bernardo, looked down at him. "I got a score to settle with you," he said. "You didn't give me your math homework like I told you and I got in trouble. Now *you're* in for trouble." He raised his fist.

"I don't want to fight. Get out of here."

"Get out of here," James mimicked. "You Chicanos got no guts. Let's see if you got any blood." Bernardo ducked, but the fist slammed against his ear. Tears sprang to his eyes, half pain, half anger.

"Chicky Chicano!" James sneered. "You ain't worth messing with." He turned and left.

That's when the idea came to Bernardo. An idea bigger than the raw pain in his ear. He'd show Cleary he had guts. He'd show everyone.

Now Bernardo listened to the Chevy edge down the driveway. It was almost time. By tonight, all the kids would know he was no chicken!

The kitchen windows let in a rainy morning light. Bernardo slipped quietly into his chair. Mama was at the stove.

"Eggs and peppers for you, Bernardo?"

"No, I'll have this," he answered, reaching for the box of Kellogg's. Eggs and peppers were too Mexican for today.

Mama noticed the flash of excitement cross his face as he thought of what the day would bring. She studied him. "What is it with you this morning?" she asked.

Bernardo thought quickly. His mother often read his mind like she read the morning paper.

"I'm glad it's Friday," he offered. "No school tomorrow."

"Always glad to get out of a little work." Mama smiled as she said it. She knew that Saturday was no vacation for her son. He worked all morning at the Tortilla Kitchen and helped with chores all afternoon at home.

Bernardo changed the subject. "Mama, do you think

it will rain all day?" A small worry pulled at him. What if they cancelled everything because of rain!

"I don't think so," Mama answered. "But you wear your slicker anyway. I don't want you sitting all day in wet clothes." She picked up the paper and sat across from him with her cup of coffee.

Bernardo didn't want to be bothered with his heavy slicker. But he couldn't think of a good reason for saying so, other than telling the truth. This was one time Mama would not want to hear the truth.

"He's such a handsome man," she said half to herself. "And she's so beautiful."

"Who?" Bernardo asked. He knew who.

"The President and Jackie," Mama answered. "It will be a jungle downtown today. They'll be blocking all the streets. Right around lunchtime, too. It says here that some schools are closing today so the kids can get a look at Kennedy as he rides by," she continued. "Too bad you won't be able to do that."

Bernardo choked on a swallow of milk.

"Here. Wipe your mouth," Mama said, handing him a napkin. "Why would Father Boyle keep the parish school open today?" she went on. "Kennedy, the first Catholic president and all. I think Father Boyle must be a Republican!" she said.

Bernardo slurped the last milk from his bowl.

"Bernardo!" Mama scolded.

"It's getting late, Mama," he reminded her. "I've got to go."

"Oh, boy!" she said, eyeing the clock. "Get! Get! If school calls, I won't be here to tell them you're just a slowpoke on your way."

Bernardo knew this. He had figured it into his plan. On Friday, Mama cleaned house for old Uncle Felipe. This house would be empty when the phone rang. And it would ring. It would ring because today Bernardo was not going to school! He was going to see President Kennedy!

Risking It

As Bernardo walked out into the rain, he went over his plan. First he had to get rid of his books. Outside the Tortilla Kitchen was an old woodbin. It was the perfect place. His books would be waiting for him when he went back there later. He could pick them up, walk into the restaurant, and look as if he had just come from school.

Without his books, he could move fast. He'd get away from the Kitchen quickly and circle back to a bus stop on the Boulevard. Buses to Dealey Plaza ran every ten minutes this time of day. Everyone was heading to the Plaza today. That's where he'd go.

He splatted through the quiet morning, zigzagging across lots, staying out of everyone's way. It wouldn't do to have some kid see him walking *away* from school. Bernardo pictured himself telling the kids how Kennedy looked. Maybe he'd call Santo tonight. And wait until James Cleary found out! Thinking about him made Bernardo's blood boil. The bully! Picking on kids because their folks had come from Mexico. It didn't matter to him that they were American citizens.

Well, who was the best American now? Who had the guts to *skip school* just to prove it? I'll really rub it in, thought Bernardo. He grinned. He thought of Maria Elena Cruz and grinned some more. She once told him she liked his wavy hair. He wondered if she liked boys who had guts.

Bernardo started to run. He felt good. His plan was surefire. Mama and Papa would think he was in school. His teacher would think he was sick at home.

There was only one thing that could go wrong. A *big* thing. If Papa should catch him hiding his books at the restaurant, it would be the worst day of his life. It would be worse than James Cleary slamming him in the ear.

He'd get it from Papa for skipping school and for lying. Worse than that, Papa would probably drag him back to St. Anna's. The teacher would know he skipped. The whole class would know he got caught. And James Cleary would know. That was the worst!

"I can't get caught. I'm *not* going to get caught," Bernardo said to himself. But thinking about it made his hands sweat. The woodbin was in the alley. To get to it, Bernardo would have to pass the double doors of the work kitchen. They were always open, even in November, to let the air move about and cool things down. Bernardo's stomach did flips.

He neared the barbershop on the corner. One more block to go. The barber's was still closed. Its red, white, and blue pole was not turning.

"What's the matter with you?" Bernardo said to the pole, bumping it with his shoulder. "Don't you know what today is? Why do you have our flag's colors if you're not going to get excited about a president's visit?"

Bernardo peeked around the hood of his slicker to see if anyone noticed him talking to a barber pole. The street was empty except for a car going in the opposite direction. He laughed out loud, silly with adventure. So far everything had gone as planned. Why sweat?

It had stopped raining. Bernardo moved on toward the restaurant. Papa had hired family from Mexico to help there. His cousin, Luiz, would be at the stove, sizzling meat for breakfast. Ignez, Luiz's sister, would be mixing tortilla dough or cutting chilies for lunch.

With a little luck, Papa would be busy talking to customers in the dining room.

As Bernardo neared the alley, the scent of onions and sweet vinegar tickled his nose. Walk slower, he told himself. Be careful. Voices and laughter mixed with the hiss of running water. He moved, catlike, toward the open double doors. He could hear them all. Luiz. Ignez. And, oh no, Papa.

Papa's voice came closer. Bernardo closed his eyes and pushed himself against the outside wall. "Where's that crate of celery?" Papa's words boomed from just inside the door.

"Ah, here it is," he answered himself. Bernardo could see his father's shadow bend over to pull the crate from under a long wooden table.

"It's good everyone decided to make deliveries early today." Papa breathed hard as he lifted the big double crate of celery. "The market would be stuck with all their fresh vegetables if they couldn't deliver them until after the President passes through. Here, Ignez, be sure you wash this good. We don't want customers with muck in their teeth." The dining room door squeaked as Papa walked out of the kitchen.

"Just once," Ignez complained after him. "I wish he'd give me credit for knowing how to wash a vegetable." She slammed the crate against the sink. By the time the racket was over, Bernardo had passed to the other side of the double door.

Breathing hard, he scurried to the woodbin and lifted the lid. It was dusty but dry. He put his books in the bottom and quietly closed the lid. Like a shadow, he doubled back. In seconds, he was at the corner, waiting for the bus.

Traffic was in its early morning rush and people were going everywhere. Bernardo melted in. He had done it! His plan was working. This was going to be the best day of his life, not the worst!

As he waited for the bus, he slipped out of the slicker. The coolness of November slid through his sweater.

He'd taken money for bus fare from Mama's purse last night. It was the first time he'd stolen anything. But he couldn't think about that now. A dime going and a dime coming home. Only twenty cents. He prayed Mama wouldn't notice. He'd tell Father Boyle in confession. God would understand. As the bus came, the sun came out. Maybe God was helping.

Shots from Somewhere

The bus turned onto the Boulevard. Bernardo settled back. It was nine o'clock. The President's plane would land at Love Air Field just before noon.

A map in last night's paper showed how the motorcade would get from the airport to the Trademart, the place where the President would have lunch. He would be going by Dealey Plaza a little after twelve o'clock. Plenty of time, Bernardo thought.

A man got on the bus and sat next to Bernardo.

His jacket smelled like car grease. He smiled. "School closed today?" he asked.

Bernardo nodded. It wasn't all a lie. Some schools were closed.

"Well, this is a big day for Dallas," he went on. "You're probably too young to understand this, but when I look at our President, I feel as if everything is going to be all right with the world. He's young. He's smart. He's rich, too. That helps, doesn't it?" He laughed.

Bernardo smiled.

"Yeah," the man continued. "He's a leader! He makes you want to do things. What'd he say? Ask not about the country . . . ? Whatever!"

Bernardo knew the quote by heart. "He said 'Ask not what your country can do for you; ask what you can do for your country.' "

The man looked at Bernardo. "Yeah, that's it. Smart kid!" The praise felt good. "This country needed someone like JFK to give it a boost," the man went on. "And Jackie, too. She sure helps to polish things up! Makes me proud to be an American."

Bernardo felt he should say something. "I hope they like Dallas," he offered.

"What's not to like about Dallas?" The man grinned. "I just hope they don't forget us after today is over."

The bus rattled along. Bernardo thought about the

Kennedys. Social Studies was boring, but learning about the First Family was different. It was fun.

Some kids in class had Kennedy scrapbooks. Papa helped Bernardo with his. Often at work he'd hear of something that John-John or Caroline had done. He'd write it down for Bernardo's book. Papa thought JFK was the best!

Suddenly the bus pulled over. "This is as far as we go today, folks," said the driver. "Sorry. Everything up ahead is closed off for the President's visit." He opened the doors.

The man patted Bernardo's knee. "Have a good time, kiddo," he said and got up to leave. Bernardo got off the bus, also.

Large buildings were everywhere. Traffic inched along. Sidewalks were packed with people. Bernardo shifted the slicker on his arm.

Up ahead, he heard the roar of a street-cleaning machine and saw a pile of wooden traffic fences. He couldn't believe his eyes. Dealey Plaza. This was it. He was here!

A bank clock said 9:30. People were wandering about the Plaza, looking for the best place to watch. Bernardo crossed Elm Street and found a spot on the curb. Two policemen on motorcycles rode up and down, looking things over.

It feels like a holiday, he thought. Back at school, the kids would be finishing math now. Bernardo felt a little guilty. But more than that, he felt smart. Smarter than his teacher, smarter than all his classmates who were still in school. And *much* smarter than James Cleary!

The morning went on. The crowd began to thicken. A loud voice startled Bernardo. "You're gonna have to move, buddy." The buttons and badge of a policeman glinted in the sun. "Can't stay here," he said. "We need this space for the TV crew." A van was unloading gear nearby.

"Okay," Bernardo said. He looked around for another good place. Across the street was a white building. In front of it was a grassy knoll. "Is that okay?" he asked, pointing.

"Yeah, sure," the policeman answered.

Bernardo crossed over. The grass was still damp and chilly. He folded his slicker and sat on it. This is great, he thought. Much better. From where he sat, he could look up the street and see the place where Main Street joined Elm. He'd see when the motorcade turned the corner.

The clock said 11:40. Workers in nearby office buildings were taking early lunch, eating sandwiches outdoors on the grass. Bernardo looked around. Not many Latinos in this crowd. It felt strange. A family with a small baby and a blond, teenaged daughter had spread a blanket next to him.

"Hi," the girl said.

"Hi," he answered.

"This is terrific, isn't it?" she said.

"Uh-huh," he answered, surprised that she would talk to him. He wasn't her age and he wasn't Anglo.

"Are you a Kennedy fan?" she asked.

"Yeah," he answered, thinking of his scrapbook. "I know lots of stories about him."

"Oh, yeah? Like what?" The girl seemed interested.

"Like when he was in the Navy in World War Two and got a medal." Bernardo lost some of his shyness. "My father said he swam through water with sharks and everything to save some sailors who were drowning."

"I knew about the medal, but I never knew about the sharks." The girl looked amazed.

"It's true. I even have a model of his boat, PT 109." Bernardo kept the model on his dresser in front of the big mirror.

"That's neat," she said. The girl picked up her baby sister. "I think Jackie is terrific, don't you?" She jiggled the baby on her knees.

To Bernardo, Jackie, with her big brown eyes, looked a little bit like Mama.

"It was tough when their little son Patrick died," the girl said. "They were so broken up."

Bernardo nodded. "Just like ordinary people, you know, like one of us," he said, watching the baby bounce and giggle.

The girl looked hard at Bernardo. "Yeah," she said, as if she'd never thought of that.

It was after 12:00. A patrol car rode up and down, sweeping people back onto the sidewalks.

"Do you know what that place is?" the girl asked, pointing to a large building near the corner. "It's the School Book Depository. Yuck!"

"What's that?" Bernardo asked.

"It's where *all* our textbooks are stored."

The word *school* edged against Bernardo's thoughts, but only for a minute. He noticed that one window, way up, was open.

The girl's mother took the baby and gave her a bottle. "Offer your young friend something to eat," she said to her daughter.

The girl had sandwiches in a paper sack. "Want one?" she asked.

Bernardo was hungry. When she put the sandwich in his hand, he took it. "Thank you," he said.

Peanut butter and jelly. Very American! Eating peanut butter and jelly today was almost patriotic.

"Look at those two," the girl said, swallowing her food and pointing with her head.

A man with a movie camera balanced himself on a wide marble railing. "Hang on to my shirt, would you?" he said to a woman behind him.

The woman laughed. "What would you do without

me, Mr. Zapruder?" He focused the camera as she hung on. People smiled.

Bernardo finished the last of his sandwich. He ran his tongue around the peanut-buttery taste still in his mouth and lifted his face to the sun. Life couldn't be better, he thought.

In the distance, people had begun to cheer. The crowd stood up, straining to see. "Here, get in front of me," the girl said. "Okay?"

"Uh-huh." He had a perfect, unblocked view of the corner. Motorcycles with revved-up engines made the turn. Behind them came city officials and their wives. Secret Service men stood on the cars' running boards, their sunglasses like mirrors as they turned their heads from left to right, searching the area. Everyone was smiling and waving.

"There they are! There they are!" yelled the girl as a dark convertible rounded the corner. "I recognize Jackie."

Bernardo recognized her, too, in her pink jacket and little round hat. She carried red roses. Next to her sat the President. His smile dazzled the crowd and the crowd roared. In the front seat was the governor of Texas, John Connally. He and Mrs. Connally looked proud.

Bernardo was speechless. His smile stretched his face from corner to corner.

The black car moved slowly, almost stopping directly in front of Bernardo. Bernardo waved furiously. President Kennedy turned, looked right at him, smiled grandly and waved back. A sound cracked the air.

Why was the President staring at him? How strange. Then he bent forward. Something was wrong. Another crack. Bernardo felt a *whizz* of heat fly by his cheek. At the same moment, the President's head flew back in a burst of blood.

The world screamed in Bernardo's ears. He felt himself thrown to the ground. He tasted the soft grass as his mouth pressed against the earth. The girl sheltered him with her body. He struggled to get free.

"Let me up," he gasped, pushing her off. Sirens screeched. People were running in all directions. Bernardo stood. The motorcade was flying down the street, as if someone had speeded up an old film. He gaped at the place where seconds before the President had smiled at him.

His eyes followed the motorcade. Where were they going? He couldn't believe what he had seen. "Come back!" he screamed at the fleeing cars. "Come back! Come back!"

A Secret
for Keeping

The girl's mother yelled, "Come on, come on. Let's get out of here!" The girl looked at Bernardo, terror on her face. Then she followed her mother.

Bernardo stood by himself. He began walking, slowly, following the sidewalk wherever it went.

Around him people were talking, crying, pointing. He didn't understand what they said. He only knew that the President had been shot.

Don't let him die, Bernardo prayed. Let him live. Let him live. The fierce, bloody picture filled his mind.

He wanted to run home. To tell Mama and Papa. But he couldn't. They thought he was at school! He wandered about.

Traffic seemed hushed now, dream cars in a nightmare, moving slowly, as if they didn't want to go wherever they were going. A light turned red just as Bernardo was about to cross a street. He waited. A car with its windows down stopped next to him. Words from its radio punched into the street . . . "President Kennedy was pronounced dead at 1:00 this afternoon. The President was killed by a gunshot wound to the head."

The driver of the car put her head against the steering wheel. Bernardo froze. By the time he was able to cross the street, the light had again turned red.

"Bernardo, where have you been?" His mother came toward him, white with worry.

"Walking."

His father pushed through the dining room door into the restaurant kitchen. Relief filled his face when he saw his son. "There you are! It's 6:30. Why didn't you come right here from school?"

Bernardo opened his mouth to speak, but closed it again. He didn't have the energy to make up a lie. He didn't have the courage to tell the truth.

"Where have you been?" his mother repeated.

Something about Bernardo held back her anger.

"Just walking."

Mama frowned at Papa.

"Come here, Bernardo." Papa put his arm around his son. "You've heard about our President?"

Bernardo buried his head in his father's apron. He didn't need to answer.

"This has been a bad day for our country," Papa said. "And it has been a bad day for you. I know. I know." But Papa didn't know about his skipping school. Guilt tightened Bernardo's insides.

"What has happened is awful. Awful," Papa went on. "Impossible to understand. But the Kennedys, they are a strong family. You will see. They will handle this like soldiers. We must try to do the same. There is a reason for everything. Come, Bernardo, have some supper."

"I'm not hungry, Papa."

"No? Well, maybe in a little while."

Mama looked at Bernardo. "Where is your slicker?" she asked.

Bernardo panicked. "I left it . . ." he began.

"You left it at school!" Mama interrupted. "I hope it keeps the cloak hall warm and dry." She tried to make him feel better. But he felt miserable. Mama was making up lies he hadn't even thought of. Things were getting worse by the minute.

Suddenly the spicy kitchen smells were too much for Bernardo. "I don't feel so good," he said. "Can I go home?"

"Dolores, go with him," Papa said. "There's not so much to do here. I think we'll close early. People are so busy with what's on TV, they don't even know what they're eating."

"Okay," Mama agreed, as she took off her apron. "Good idea."

That evening, Bernardo lay in bed. He could hear TV voices filling the living room. Voices that sounded important, men mostly, reporters who were trying to understand all that had happened.

He tossed and turned. Papa's words kept burning in his mind. "There is a reason for everything," he had said. Bernardo wasn't sure how, but he had a feeling the reason for the shooting had something to do with him.

What he did today was a bad idea. He wasn't such a great American after all. Oh, he had wanted to see the President, all right. But what he had really wanted to do was to show up James Cleary, even if it meant lying and stealing to do it.

For the millionth time, Bernardo relived the shooting. The President waved to him. He smiled at him. Then he was shot. Could it have been Bernardo's fault?

Was God angry with him for hating James and for the lying and the stealing? Was this part of his punishment?

"What can I do?" Bernardo asked himself. The night seemed to say, "You can do nothing. It's too late to say you're sorry. You can never tell. It's your secret forever." Misery washed through him. He tucked it deep inside himself and, at last, sleep closed him in.

Not Even Santo

"Here, Bernardo, do the baseboards." Papa handed his son a basin of sudsy water. "Keep yourself busy. It will take your mind off things."

Bernardo took the water and went into the dining room. It was Saturday morning. The Tortilla Kitchen was closed for its weekly cleaning.

It usually made Bernardo feel good to do his part at the restaurant. But not today. He crept along on his hands and knees behind tables and around booths, scrubbing as he went.

Santo had come to watch him work. He followed Bernardo around. "You know, you're lucky you're little and can get in those small places," he said. Santo was tall and skinny, like his four brothers.

"Uh-huh," Bernardo murmured. He did not look up.

"They say the President was a tall man—over six feet!"

Bernardo breathed deeply. Santo went on. "I shouldn't say 'the President.' Johnson is the President now. Did you see him get sworn in?"

"Uh-uh."

"It was on the plane when they were bringing Kennedy's body back to Washington, D.C. Jackie was there, too. They said her suit was all bloody."

Bernardo plunged his rag into the soapy water and squeezed it out.

"They took Kennedy to Bethesda Naval Hospital for an autopsy. That's when they take the body apart to see everything."

"For gosh sakes, Santo. Do you have to keep talking about it like that?" Bernardo sat back on his heels and wiped his forehead.

"I'm just telling you what happened! You don't seem to know much about anything."

"I went to bed early, that's why." Bernardo crept along the floor.

"Oh, that's right, you were sick yesterday."

Bernardo scrubbed harder.

"Do you feel better today?" Santo asked.

"I don't feel that good, to tell you the honest truth."
How good it felt to tell the honest truth.

"Oh. Sorry. You know they brought the body to the
White House in the middle of the night and they put
it in a room with candles. There were people there
kind of keeping an eye on things."

"It was an honor guard," Bernardo said. The story
had been on TV that morning. Bernardo remembered
the reporter telling what a privilege it was to be chosen
for honor guard. One had to have character. *I'd* never
get picked, he thought. His secret felt like a ball of
lead.

"They caught the guy who did it, you know." Santo
was filled with his news.

"I know."

"His name is Lee Harvey Oswald. He did it from
the Book Depository. He shot from the sixth-floor window."

Bernardo remembered the hot flash whizzing by his
right cheek. The Book Depository had been down the
street to his left. He stopped scrubbing and looked
puzzled.

"What's the matter?" Santo asked.

"Are you sure?"

"Am I sure about what?"

"Are you sure about where the shot came from?"

"Yeah, I'm sure. They found the gun and everything. Some man in a shoe store said he saw this guy hanging around, acting suspicious. It was Oswald. They followed him to the Texas Theater. They got him, and guess what?"

"What?"

"He works at the Book Depository! They think he shot a policeman, too."

Santo went on and on. Bernardo stopped listening. His whole attention turned to what had happened yesterday. The scene came back with a force that almost knocked him over. But something was puzzling. He was certain that shots had come from another direction.

"Bernardo!"

Bernardo jumped. Santo had yelled his name right in his ear. "What?" he yelled back.

"I *said*, what do you think John-John and Caroline are thinking?"

Bernardo dropped his rag and stood up. "For gosh sakes, what do you think they're thinking? They're probably all shook up!" he screamed. "It's their father, for gosh sakes."

"Hey, don't get so excited! What's the matter with you, anyway?"

Bernardo turned away to hide the tears. "Nothing."

"I guess you feel bad. I know he was your hero."

"I'm sorry, Santo," Bernardo answered. If only he

could tell his friend the whole story. "Santo, I—" No. He couldn't tell. Not even Santo. "Look, I think I'm going to quit now. It's almost 10:30. Why don't you call me later, okay?"

"Yeah, sure, Bernardo. What're you going to do?"

"I don't know. Go home and lie down, maybe."

"Jeez, I hope you're not getting sick all over again."

Bernardo cringed inside. "I don't think so," he said.

"Well, so long. See you later, alligator."

"Yeah, see you, Santo."

Bernardo sat on his bed looking through the scrapbook. Here was Jackie's picture the night she became the First Lady. She looked like Cinderella in her white party dress and cape. And here was the President, making a speech on a cold day. His breath turned to smoke. Here he was in uniform during World War II, commanding his torpedo boat, and at the Berlin Wall, being cheered by the German people.

Another picture showed Jackie and John Kennedy coming home from the hospital with their new baby, John-John. Another showed him standing alone, after learning that their newest baby, Patrick, had died. The picture Bernardo liked best was one of JFK sailing, near his home in Hyannis Port, Massachusetts. He was smiling into the sun, the wind picking up his hair as if to lift him away. Looking at this picture, Bernardo promised himself that one day, he, too, would learn to sail.

When Papa first saw Bernardo's scrapbook, he had said, "Someday you will show this to your children and your grandchildren. They'll be amazed to think that you and this very special man were alive at the same time." Bernardo didn't know how he felt about being a grandpa, but he knew how he felt about John F. Kennedy.

"Papa, did you live when Lincoln was alive?" he had asked. Papa's laugh filled the room. "Lincoln lived in the last century."

"Oh. Yeah. Well, did you live when *anybody* special was alive?"

"Sure. And there she is!" Papa pointed to Mama.

Mama threw the dish towel at him. "Be special yourself and dry a dish." She had laughed. Bernardo loved it when Mama and Papa teased each other. It made things seem so good.

Bernardo tossed back on the bed. Things would never be good again.

The Head in
the Mirror

Sunday morning arrived like an enemy. It was almost time for church. Bernardo knew he couldn't stay in bed forever. Mama was beginning to suspect that he wasn't really sick. He rolled out of bed and got ready.

There were a lot of people in church today. More than usual. Instead of sending their wives, the men came, too. Everyone had the same look of sadness. Bernardo wondered if God noticed he was there.

Father Boyle began to talk about the President's

death. Bernardo put his head down in his hands and pushed his thumbs into his ears. Mama poked him. "Are you sick?"

"No."

"Then sit up straight!"

Bernardo sat up. That's when he noticed James Cleary, sitting next to his father. Mr. Cleary was a tall man. Beside him, James didn't look so big after all.

On the way out of church, James stopped Bernardo. "Is your ear okay?" Bernardo looked baffled.

"Where I hit you. Is it okay?"

"Yeah, it's okay." Bernardo had almost forgotten.

"Too bad about Kennedy, huh?" said James. He walked away. Bernardo stared. It was the first time James had ever talked with him without picking a fight.

"Who's that?" Mama asked.

"Just a kid from school," Bernardo said. He wished he could tell his mother everything.

Later that morning, Mama served early lunch in front of the TV. Papa had come home from the Tortilla Kitchen, leaving Luiz in charge.

At City Hall, police were getting ready to move Lee Harvey Oswald to the county jail. TV cameras covered the story, sending it across the country. Police were worried that a crowd would try to grab Oswald. People were just that angry! There were guards everywhere.

At last the cameras showed a group of men moving

through a door. Lee Harvey Oswald was walking, hand-cuffed between two men. One of them wore a large white hat.

Can I tell by his face if he's really the killer, Bernardo wondered. Do people's faces show what they've done? He stared at the TV screen, waiting to see. Oswald came into full view, looking like a kid in his black sweater. He had a big bruise over his left eye.

Suddenly there was a quick movement near the bottom of the TV screen. Oswald's face became twisted, his mouth forming a perfect "O." He bent over, dragging the policemen toward the ground. Papa jumped out of his chair.

The newscaster was yelling into the microphone. "He's been shot! Lee Harvey Oswald has been shot!" The TV picture jiggled all over the screen as the cameraman tried to get out of the way. Confusion ripped over the airways. The entire nation was watching a man get killed on TV. In an instant, the entire nation knew the name of the man who shot him. Jack Ruby.

Papa and Mama were talking at once. The phone rang. It was Luiz. Everyone was in a frenzy. Only Bernardo didn't seem to care. He sat in the chair as if he'd been turned to stone. No one seemed to notice.

In the middle of the night, Bernardo woke up all at once. He jumped out of bed. Everything was quiet. Everything was dark. Why was he so wide awake? The

glow from the streetlamp filled his room. He could see himself in the dresser mirror.

"What is it?" he asked his reflection. It stared back at him. He let his breath out and sat on the bed, remembering.

"What am I going to do?" he asked himself. He looked at the mirror again. Only his head shone above the top of the dresser. It seemed to be sitting there by itself.

Weird, thought Bernardo. I *am* weird. I'm weird to think all of this is my fault! How could it be my fault? Other kids skip school and nothing like this happens.

He looked at his head in the mirror. It stared back at him. "I didn't mean to do anything wrong," he said out loud.

The head in the mirror stared back. Bernardo leaned into the edge of the bed with the back of his legs. "I didn't mean it! I didn't mean it!" he shouted at the mirror. With a wail he threw himself back on the bed. The head in the mirror disappeared.

The hall light flashed on. Papa was in the doorway, his pajama top crooked on his shoulders. "Bernardo? Hey, hey, Bernardo," he said, gathering him up. "You're having a bad dream, eh?"

Bernardo couldn't answer. He sobbed into his father's chest. Papa hugged him. "It's just a dream," he said.

"No, it's not," Bernardo cried.

"What's wrong?" Mama stood in the doorway, the light making a shadow of her body.

"He's just having a bad dream," Papa said.

Bernardo squirmed away from his father.

"No, I'm not!" he insisted.

"Bernardo, it's a nightmare," Mama said. "God knows with all that's happened these three days, we should all be having nightmares."

"It's not a dream, Mama." Bernardo stood up. His voice got louder and louder. "You don't know! It's not—" He stopped. Papa stared, waiting. Mama, too.

It was then, that his secret exploded into the room. "I was *there*, Papa. I saw it. And it was my fault."

Papa's mouth dropped open. His face wrinkled with confusion. He looked at Mama to see if she understood.

"What are you talking about, Bernardo?" she asked.

His words chopped their way through his crying as he tried to tell his parents. "I—saw—Kennedy's—head—get—shot off."

"I knew we shouldn't have had that TV on so much," Mama declared.

"Mama!" Bernardo stamped his foot. "I skipped school. I was *there*. I saw it happen! The President smiled at me and then—."

In the silence, the clock chimed half past the hour. No one spoke. Bernardo wept quietly, looking from

Mama to Papa. "I did things to make God angry," he said softly. "That's why He let it happen when the President smiled at me."

Papa moved over and made room on the bed. He pulled Bernardo down next to him and patted the mattress. "Sit down, Dolores," he said to his wife. "We have a long story to hear."

When the Drums Stopped

Something about the day felt like a holiday. Every store and school was closed. No banks did business. There was no mail. But it was no holiday. Today was President Kennedy's funeral.

Everyone was glued to the TV, listening to the steady beat of drums. Everyone chilled at the sight of the black horse with the backwards stirrups, following the President's body. There was no rider. There were no words, no songs, just the rhythmic pounding of drums.

Santo sat with Bernardo on the floor of Bernardo's

living room. After he had found out about Bernardo skipping school, he began asking questions. So many questions that Bernardo finally told him he didn't want to talk about it.

"When do you think you'll feel like talking about it?" Santo asked, as he stared at the TV.

"I don't know, Santo. Not just yet. It bothers me."

"Okay. But promise me something?"

"What?"

"The next time you skip school, take me with you?"

"Sure, Santo." It wasn't hard to make this promise. Bernardo knew there'd *never* be a next time. He caught Papa's eye. Papa winked.

"Hey, look there," Santo called, pointing to the screen. "John-John's saluting."

"Poor baby," Mama said softly. "What a way to celebrate your birthday." John-John Kennedy was three years old today.

"I wouldn't call him poor. He's got millions of bucks!"

"Santo, there are lots of ways of being poor," Mama answered. "He has no Papa."

Bernardo knew just what Mama meant. He looked at his own father and remembered how quietly he had listened the other night as Bernardo told his secret. When he had gotten to the part about making God angry, Papa closed his eyes and shook his head.

"No, no, no," he had said softly. "Bernardo, the

God I know doesn't punish young boys. Do you know what He does?" He looked deep into his son's brown eyes. "God lets parents take care of that." Mama smiled.

Then strong arms pulled him close. He felt his father's breath in his hair. "What's happened is not a punishment," Papa said. "It's just the way life is. Something happens. Why? We don't know, exactly. Sometimes we can figure out the little reasons. Almost never can we figure out the big reason."

The night had folded quietly around them. Bernardo looked at Mama. "What will my punishment be?" he asked.

She glanced at Papa. They had a conversation without words, the way parents do. "I think, Bernardo, you have been punished enough," she said.

The reporter's voice was whispery as he described all that was happening. The funeral procession had walked from St. Matthew's Cathedral, across the Potomac River to Arlington National Cemetery. The First Lady was dressed all in black. A veil covered her face. She walked between the President's two brothers, Bobby and Ted. They all stood at the grave.

When the drums stopped, the world shrank into silence. Then silence became filled with the sound of taps, clear and sad. Navy jet fighters flew overhead in a fly-by salute. One plane left the squadron. It meant that a great man had left this world. Guns were fired. Prayers were said. The flag covering the President's casket was folded and given to Mrs. Kennedy. A flame was lighted, meant to burn forever.

And it was done. Papa turned off the TV. He looked at Bernardo and Santo. "Would you like to come to the Kitchen with me?"

"I thought you were going to keep the restaurant closed all day," Mama said.

"I was. But maybe people need a place to go, to be with each other. To help each other forget."

"And to help each other remember," Bernardo said.

ABOUT THIS BOOK

Camelot! The name makes us think of kings and queens, of magic, and of dreams come true. In 1960, when John Fitzgerald Kennedy and Jacqueline Bouvier Kennedy became President and First Lady of the land, many felt that Camelot had come to America. Dreams *would* come true.

Jack and Jackie. How they were loved! People gobbled up Kennedy gossip like dessert. JFK's smile was everywhere—on mantels, in gas stations, in wallets. He and Jackie were heroes of the day, rich and beautiful. For many adults, those memories remain strong today. In writing this book, I viewed films, read newspapers, books, and magazines, and talked to people who, like myself, remembered well.

It's hard to say why so many people felt as they did about our thirty-fifth president. Perhaps because his father, an ambassador to Great Britain, and his mother, a Boston socialite, were exciting people. Perhaps it was because of his bravery in the war. Perhaps because he was so young, the youngest *ever* to be president.

On Inauguration Day, 1961, he was 44 years old.

With his power and charm, Kennedy helped people believe that the world could be a better place. He called everyone to join him in "The New Frontier." He inspired everyone to feel a love for our country. Peace Corps volunteers went to foreign lands to help others to a better life because of him.

Kennedy led with courage. He wrote a book called *Profiles in Courage,* about men and women who lived brave lives. When Russia put war missiles in Cuba, only 90 miles from our country, he was ready to challenge Russia to war. Kennedy worked with Dr. Martin Luther King, Jr., the great civil rights leader, to solve racial problems. He encouraged NASA to work toward sending an American to the moon.

Although most people felt that JFK was doing good things for our country, some did not. Today, it is suspected that Oswald was not the only person involved in the President's death, that others wanted him dead. Mr. Abraham Zapruder is more than a character in this story. He is a real person who took a real movie. The movie shows that other shots may have come from the front of the motorcade. Many are studying the facts again to see if there was a conspiracy. In any case, bullets in Dallas took the life of a very special man one November noon.

—V.T.G.